THE
Unforgettable

BOOK 1

Dr. Z

PAGE PUBLISHING
Conneaut Lake, PA

First originally published by Page Publishing 2024

ISBN 979-8-88960-619-2 (pbk)
ISBN 979-8-88960-626-0 (digital)

Printed in the United States of America

PART 1

ZVMCX AND DR. Z

C H A P T E R 1

THE STRANGE BEGINNING

Zvmcx is on a city rooftop. With determination and readiness, knowing full well that this is the only way to put an end to what he's done, he approaches the edge and jumps off, plummeting to the ground beneath him.

* * * * *

Zvmcx, a seemingly homeless man who is down on his luck already, is getting beaten up and harassed by a group of thugs who found him in an alley. Suddenly, like a switch was just flipped, in a flash of complex movements, he is able to defend himself, countering each attack with such speed and agility that he himself is not used to. He pauses for a moment, confused at his newly found capability. The band of thugs are just as confused. Zvmcx walks away from the altercation, quickly leaving the group dazed on the floor. Unbeknownst to him, a shadowy figure watches him from the corner of the alley. Stuck deep in his contemplation, Zvmcx continues walking without a word to anyone.

The following day, he returns to his street side to continue his daily routine, begging for change. The day of change collection is rough for him with the highlight only being a few quarters, and the worst, the used condoms being thrown in his cup. Time revolves

3

around him being treated like a trash can, being hit with used tissues and empty chip bags, taking whatever he gets that is usable currency into the bodega. Luckily for him he can afford his favorite treat, a donut. There are whispers in the background of sly comments. The "ew" or "I can't believe they let him in here" at first is saddening, but this becomes commonplace as he's grown used to it.

After buying his donut, he leaves.

Upon leaving, Zvmcx sees the same group of people that tried beating him up the previous day, attempting to rob someone. Thinking about the new fighting skills he miraculously acquired, he goes in to save the day. He doesn't. For some unknown reason, his newly acquired fighting skills do not kick in. He pauses, frightened and confused. The young group of thugs take advantage of the situation and begin beating him to enact revenge for the previous day— this time, in return, leaving Zvmcx on the floor beaten.

After awakening, he stumbles away, finding a hose to wash himself off. He goes onward to a familiar alley, and he sees another bum. Feeling a little more at ease because he is finally in the presence of someone that understands his day-to-day struggle, Zvmcx gives a gentle wave as he walks past but is suddenly tripped, falling face-first. The other homeless man runs off deeper in the alley. Zvmcx gets up, his face riddled with frustration and gives chase. As the other man turns the corner, Zvmcx does the same. When Zvmcx reaches the corner, however, there's no one to be seen. Looking upward, seeing the fire escape is pulled down and running over to the fire escape, he jumps grabbing it and begins his ascent. Reaching the rooftop, he sees nothing but a graffiti-filled wall. Walking toward the edge of the rooftop, a hand reaches out of the graffiti and grabs Zvmcx by his coat and pulls him into the graffiti.

Awakening dazed and confused, "Where the fuck am I?" he utters. Soon after that statement, he falls through the floor beneath smacking into another floor. Reasonably, he freaks out as the scenery changes. His surroundings, while structurally remain similar, are now all black and white.

Pointing to a group of mimes who sit there in front of him, "Who are you guys?" he says, suddenly getting smacked in the head as their apparent leader puts a finger over his lips and makes a "shhh" gesture. While some of these mimes have the classic stripe shirt of a mime, they are topped with a fancier overcoat. *They look like old mobsters,* Zvmcx thinks.

Another mime seems to charade to the leader. "He doesn't know the customs of this place."

The leader responds, "Are you sure this is him then?"

The other mime nods his head in reassurance. The leader approaches Zvmcx and speaks verbally. This shocks Zvmcx and the group of mimes themselves.

"You dare cross the path to challenge the Mime Gang Crew," he says.

In shock of the situation at hand, Zvmcx responds crudely, "Who the fuck is the Mime Gang Crew? Are you some new break dance group?" The leader teleports behind him. Zvmcx feels a hand on his shoulder, despite seeing no physical hand, freaking him out even further.

"You have five years to figure out who you are going to be. To study the five different arts and become who you need to be."

Zvmcx, looking utterly confused at everyone but without a moment's notice, gets quickly thrown into the first part of training—blindsight. They place a blindfold over his eyes.

For one year straight, he was blindfolded. Blindfolded as he ate, drank, showered, and fought. Teaching him to hear what cannot be seen. After what seemed like an eternity of him getting beat up, he finally starts catching on and can really defend himself while not being able to see.

After the year ended, they remove the blindfold in a dimly lit room so as to not hurt his eyes so much. The mimes in the room are audibly clapping, but their hands weirdly don't make contact. While they prepare for the second year of training, a mime reaches over Zvmcx's ears as if placing ear muffs. He still sees the contactless clapping, but as the mime's hands go over his ears, he can no longer hear anything. He reaches for his ears feeling nothing, piecing together the mimes' powers, realizing they can physically alter their reality by what they mime. Now, the lesson is to feel what you cannot hear. As they use their powers to move things behind and around Zvmcx, he has to feel what's going around him to stop from being struck.

Three more years of this style of training, one for each of the five senses, Zvmcx feels like a new man. Getting to truly test and learn his limits and capabilities has boosted his confidence greatly and his sense of self, learning how to hear and even charade in mime himself.

"Are you ready?" The leader mimes to him.

"I think I am." He mimes back.

After leaving the fortress that they've been hauled up in for so long, Zvmcx goes to an area of all sand. A "beach" if you will, but the sandy floor is actually salt. The black sand-like salt lay on his feet and the gray sky stands above. He begins walking alone, but his stride is no longer the same. Along this journey of what seems like miles, the mimes cut him telekinetically starting at his ankles. Though what's this? His wounds are not closing black. The mimes are in shock. This has never happened before. He is supposed to turn into a mime, but his flesh is still in color. The mimes now stand disappointed but allow him to leave. He leaves the same way that he entered—through the graffiti on the rooftop. The world surprises him upon reentry. The world full of color is something he isn't used to anymore. The world itself, besides color, also seems different than when he left. The entire event seems so unreal. He picks himself up off the floor not truly believing what happened. *I probably just fell asleep up here,* he thinks.

Coming down from the roof, he begins walking along the sidewalk as he always had. A big white van pulls up behind him with a large NXC on the side of the van. Inside reveals a team of what looks like SWAT officers in an all-white uniform from helmet to boots. They lock Zvmcx in cuffs quickly and throw him into the van. The van stops at a tower—the "Non-Xistent Corporation."

Inside, they shuffle Zvmcx in.

"What the hell is going on?" he screams while fighting his restraints. The group of men in uniform drop into a room where a group of professional-looking individuals stands before him.

"Pardon my team if they've been rough with you, sir. The White-Out Squad tries to move with the utmost efficiency."

"Who are you guys? What the fuck is going on?" says Zvmcx.

"We are the Non-Xistent Corporation. We seemed to have lost track of your whereabouts for the last five years."

"Five years? What do you mean five years? I've just been sleeping—"

"Is that so? Okay, then would you mind just signing this sheet here?"

"No, I'm not signing anything. I don't know who you guys are. Let me go," Zvmcx says as he stands up with great triumph.

"Hmm, okay."

Back outside, it seems the mimes aren't quite done with Zvmcx. Coming out of graffiti on another building is the Mime Gang Crew. They look around, looking out of date with their old sense of style reminiscent of the '50s mafioso clothes. Infatuated by the beauty of color that the majority haven't witnessed in some time, they "ooh" at the vast color they see and "ahh" at the sound they hear. Walking further down the street, they see a crowd. The crowd of people surrounds a break-dance group. The mimes look disrespected at this display.

"Are they challenging us?" One mime "mimes" to another.

"It appears so." The leader mimes in response. They remove their coats and begin battling. The mimes begin their warm-up to martial arts moves that look like dance. One mime begins dusting his shoulders which in mime cultures show acceptance of this duel. The young dancers seeing this move imitate it believing it to just be a cool move. The mimes appear to be stunned with the audacity and look toward their leader. The leader shows a face as if to say "all right, it's on." They get into their fight stance, and in a display of acrobatic movements, one uses another to springboard their way into the air flipping. Upon landing, however, the ground ripples like water, shaking the surrounding people and scaring everyone into silence.

The leader mimes, putting his coat back on and continuing walking. "Yeah, that's what I thought."

Zvmcx is at the corner store eating a donut. Outside of the window, he sees something that he can barely believe. Yes, the mimes. It really is them, shocking Zvmcx. Spitting his coffee out in surprise, he walks outside.

"You guys are real?" he says in confusion.

"We have to go." Mimes a mime as they move to a corner alleyway.

"You guys are really real. I can't believe it," says Zvmcx.

"Are you a dumbass? Of course, we are." Mimes one of the mimes.

"Did you sign why you came back?" he continues.

"No, the ceremony wasn't completed."

"There's a reason why you're here, and we have to find out what it is."

The mimes disappear, turning into black salt falling onto the floor in front of Zvmcx.

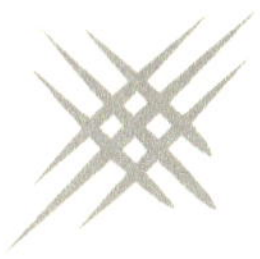

CHAPTER 2

MIMES BREAK PHYSICS

In the subway, beneath the surface of the city, a train passes through the graffiti-ridden walls. The Mime Gang Crew comes out of the graffiti before the conductor's eyes.

I definitely need to quit this shit, the conductor thinks to himself as he throws his blunt onto the floor.

The leader of the crew dusts himself off as he lands. To the right, he sees a man drumming. Entranced by the sound displayed before them, the mimes beside him begin miming the act of drumming. Sounds come out of the mimes' movements. Onlookers are looking at what appears to be invisible drums. The other mimes join in forming a drumline of sorts. A parade of onlookers soon follows the mimes all looking to record a video.

As they leave the subway grounds onto the surface of the city, the leader notices something. He sees a young boy running across the road to join the crowd, noticing a car headed straight for him as well. The leader disappears, and a sudden and large crash is heard by the crowd. The car is stopped in an instant, halting the music being played by the mimes. Everybody looks expecting the worst but sees no one there. The mother who was screaming hysterically now hears her child behind her. "Mommy, Mommy!" the young boy yells as he runs to her with open arms. The rest of the Mime Gang Crew is no longer found.

Zvmcx, once again sitting in his favorite corner store eating a donut, is watching the news.

"A child seems to magically disappear moments before being hit by a car." The reporter goes up to a witness and asks, "Tell me, sir, what did you see?"

"I don't even know, man, that was like some Chris Angel shit. They were playing music then that loud crash, and then everyone disappeared." Zvmcx runs out of the store seemingly with an understanding of who was behind sudden events.

The CEO of NXC also watches the very same news report.

"I believe we have a problem," his assistant tells him as the new report is played in the background. The CEO, a very angry man, punches a hole into his screen.

"It's starting again." As he gets up from his chair, he continues, "I need you to activate secondary protocol procedures."

"Are you sure?"

"Did I stutter? Shifty Eyes. Did I fucking stutter?"

"No, sir," his assistant utters in fear as he leaves, inputting a code into a keypad and hitting a button, activating "Shifty Eyes."

A man with an older style and swagger, sporting a skully cap with suspenders, a turtle neck, and khakis, walks into the subway station where he sees people playing a game. Three-card monte is the game they're betting on. This man decides to sit down with them. The master behind the cards begins moving the cards with great speed, but the man with eyes locks onto his target and is able to track each movement so meticulously, almost as if perceiving it in slow motion. He sees something a bit tricky.

"If you can find the right card, I'll double your bet," says the card master. The man grabs the card master's arm.

"Yeah, why don't you just give me all of it?" he says. The crowd that has been making bets is visibly irritated seeing how they've been conned and give chase to the man. The man receives a phone call. An automated voice message comes through the line.

"Hello, Shifty Eyes. Your contract has been activated. You are to retrieve information on select individuals." The name fits the man's capabilities remarkably well.

*****

Zvmcx somehow finds his way back to the NXC headquarters. He sits in front of an investigator for questioning yet again.

"I see you haven't been completely honest," says the investigator.

"What do you mean?" replies Zvmcx.

"Well, we know you know something."

"I don't know what you're talking about."

"Well, you seem to have a history of lying. Where were you at the time of the incident?"

"I don't know what you're talking about," visibly angry, Zvmcx yells in response. One of the people in the room smacks him.

"We know you're lying. We can get you to talk." There's a brief pause in the room. Zvmcx realizes what has worked before and attempts again.

"Can I leave?" he asks.

The interviewer, in shock but understanding the limitation, responds, "Yeah, you can leave. Just know we have an eye on you," as Zvmcx leaves the rooms.

Shifty Eyes is now investigating the recent scene that took place in the subway regarding the mimes.

"There's an entry point. We just have to get it when it opens," Shifty Eyes says while running his hands on the graffiti. The White-Out Squad equipped with paint rollers begins rolling paint onto the walls covering up the graffiti.

"You're not using enough paint. You have to make sure nothing is visible," he continues.

*****

Zvmcx walks to meet the Mime Gang Crew. Unbeknownst to him, Shifty Eyes is watching from a distance.

"This isn't a good time to talk." Mimes the leader of the crew, taking the graffiti door on another wall. They enter the cartoon world where the mimes originated from. A cartoon version of the city streets flows behind Zvmcx.

"Listen, there's someone out there that has a much bigger influence than you." Mimes the leader.

Zvmcx responds sharply, "Who?" The leader of the crew ignores his response and continues miming.

"You have an enemy with great power you don't understand. You have to keep an eye out. They hired someone we used to know." Popping out of another graffiti hole, they turn the corner around the block moments before the White-Out Squad covers the graffiti in white paint.

Zvmcx is now seated in an apartment—a gift from the crew— now believing that it's time he may need to see a doctor, in sheer disbelief of everything going on.

"This just can't be real," he mutters to himself while staring into a mirror. The image in the mirror changes before his eyes. An image comes through the mirror in a cloud of smoke.

"Does this seem real, you piece of shit?" He grabs Zvmcx by the neck, lifting him off the floor.

"I don't care. This isn't real," he says as he closes his eyes to deny what's in front of him. Zvmcx opens his eyes and is greeted with a quick punch by the cloudy figure.

"Does this feel real?" the figure says, knocking him out. Zvmcx finally comes to and calls his brother.

"Look, I'm exhausted, and nothing feels real. Something must be wrong."

"You say this all the time, you just have to relax. It'll be okay," his brother says in return.

Zvmcx leaves the apartment building and heads toward the train station. He hears police officers as they question a homeless man playing drums on a few buckets.

"You are being detained. We have reason to believe it was you."

"Nah, man, these demon-looking dudes came out of the wall and got the whole crowd following them playing imaginary drums."

"So you're telling me, people came out of the wall, picked up imaginary sticks, and started playing invisible drums?"

"Yes!"

"Well, we already told you, you can't play here, so you're coming anyway."

As the officers bring the man out of the subway, a young boy spray paints a graffiti tag on the wall and quickly runs away to avoid the officers. The Mime Gang Crew comes out of the newly sprayed graffiti. The leader notices something off to the side, glowing. He picks up the glowing pile and takes a sniff. The mimes look at each other. While deeper in the tunnel of the subway, they hear a cackling laugh in the distance.

CHAPTER 3

BEHIND THE CACKLING LAUGHTER

"So what is your issue with the clowns exactly?" a reporter asks the leader of the Mime Gang Crew during an interview on live TV.

"Well, in 1932, there was us and them. Our purpose was to bring joy to everyone. We were very friendly and got along well. But something changed all that. They were even welcomed to the palace," says the leader through mouthing alone as silent films play in the back, proving what he says to be true.

* * * * *

Zvmcx now walks alone until he encounters a woman. She runs up to him being the nearest person in the vicinity.

"Help me, someone stole my purse. They ran this way," says the lady. Zvmcx and the woman give chase running down the station when suddenly a light explodes onto the platform. A clown appears before them sporting a big varsity-style jacket that says on the back "Gooney Clowns." Zvmcx and the woman continue past them. The clowns begin with tricks of their own: unique dances and stunts from a jack-in-the-box style dance where they sway back and forth, looking spring-like to breathing fire. All in the confines of a subway tunnel, scaring the civilians around and calling the Mime Gang Crew to come and play. Taking a bottle of liquor, they throw it at some of the lights above.

The Mime Gang Crew suddenly appear with acrobatics, landing in a superhero pose.

The Mime Gang Crew gets into a battle position rather quickly. One in the center is ready to beat his war drums. The face-off is intense as they appear to be polar opposites. The Gooney Clowns glow brightly with fluorescent colors under the lights they just broke while mimes stand parallel from them in black and white. The leader of the mimes reminds the crew that the clowns are still family. The drummer begins to beat his drums rhythmically.

The mimes start with martial arts dance moves to shake the floor, moving the world around them with each move. The clowns mimic the mimes but in their own fashion, often stumbling for comedic effect, causing a different effect. The ground-shaking moves from the two crews cause some civilians to fall off the side of the platform, plummeting to the tracks below. The clowns throw a jack-in-the-box as it tumbles over the edge and releases a net. Catching the civilians before they hit the rails, a loud cackle from the clowns is emitted. The attention of the mimes is now garnered by the people who lay over the rails as they hear the horns roar from a train in the tunnel approaching. One of the mimes hoists his hand over his shoulders as if he is holding a bazooka. An audible *thunk* is heard as he flexes his finger, though nothing is seen. The train suddenly slows faster than the brakes could provide alone. The people scream until the train is seemingly pushed backward. It is a net of their own that the mimes launched. As the train finally ceases movement, the clowns and the mimes run at each other once again. But this time, as they run at each other, a big ball of energy that surrounds them, and they vanish.

Running down the subway steps right as the two crews vanish is Shifty Eyes and the White-Out Squad.

Pulling the people up from the nets, he utters, "What you folks just witnessed was the intro to the greatest show in Broadway today. If you have any questions, please contact your local ticket master." Pulling the last person up and taping off the area with no-entry tape, he begins investigating. He sticks his hand out and touches the paint leftover from the clowns, rubbing the salt left behind by the mimes between his fingertips and letting it fall to the floor. He snaps his fingers and orders the crew to clean up.

NXC news begins to broadcast its report on TV.

"Another phenomenon was witnessed. People are now saying they've seen two of these mysterious 'crews' in an altercation that disappeared before their eyes. A professor is here to explain what might've happened." The reporter walks over to a seemingly average professor sitting on his desk, wearing a large white lab coat, and points the mic toward his face.

"Well, I have no real solid conclusion on the events that transpired, but I speculate that perhaps a hallucinogenic gas was released to aid the spectacle that took place."

"Well, how can you explain who the people are?" asks the reporter.

"I don't know. Why you don't you try to figure it out yourself. Always asking these stupid questions. Just use Google or something," the professor says as he gets up from his chair. The projector behind him, which was showing equations and formulas, switches to Tetris.

The reporter holding her earpiece gets a message coming in. She looks at the camera and says, "We have a witness who says they know exactly who these people are."

Meanwhile, during the chase, they finally catch up to the man who stole the purse. As they approach the thief, a clean-shaven man in a lab coat with torn sleeves, and what looks to be boots, appear seemingly out of nowhere. The strange man strikes the thief in the head then sweeps the legs with a kick, making him fall on the floor. Zvmcx returns the purse to the woman.

"Who are you?" says Zvmcx.

"I'm Dr. Z," says the man.

"I like your style. Maybe we could work together," Zvmcx continues. Dr. Z doesn't respond and leaves the subway, leaving Zvmcx confused where he stands. Looking up recovering from his confusion, he sees a woman. One of the most beautiful women Zvmcx has ever seen. Walking past him, she gives him a kiss on the cheek. The amalgamation of all the events from chasing the man, meeting that stranger, and getting a kiss on the cheek from such a beautiful woman causes him to promptly and comically pass out on the floor.

The following days, as reports flew in, the NXC news broadcasts live their initial findings.

"A potential terrorist seems to be the mastermind behind the hallucinogenic gas attack earlier this week on the subway," while they show Zvmcx on the screen listed as the attacker in question. "He is now on the run. Be on the lookout for this man, but do not engage directly. Call local authorities," continues the reporter.

CHAPTER 4

AN OLD FRIEND

A member of the Mime Gang Crew runs down the alleyway while officers are not far behind him. Turning the corner, he finds a graffiti mural that he jumps into. Behind the mural reveals the cartoon world—an alternate reality that is only accessible by some. The mime sits with his back toward the common world, hearing the cops running past. He leaves the graffiti mural and begins walking, only to hear the cops have circled back, giving chase once again.

*****

A new interview is taking place live on the news, this time, featuring a member of the Gooney Clowns.

"Did he tell you what really happened in Central Park?" Pulling a TV out of nowhere, he begins to show the interviewer. "The clown in the video is wearing a…could you guess it?" A clown wearing a suit is collecting "donations" while music plays in the background.

"We were hustling or whateva," he narrates as the video shows an old woman coming to drop change in the bucket. She looks up at the clown and is greeted with a terribly grotesque wide smile. She runs off as a result. The clown on the TV is now getting pissed off. He throws the can at the woman.

"You threw a can at an innocent woman?" says the interviewer.

"Well, you're missing the point here," he says, crossing his arms. "So guess who shows up next? The Mime Gang Crew." He continues, "The Mime Gang Crew comes scratching the air like a DJ's turntable, changing the background music. How did they remix our song? See what I mean?" The clowns begin fighting with the mimes. A clown runs over to the mime and throws a right hand straight to the mime's face.

"You just punched a mime," says the reporter.

"So what? I two-pieced a mime. Go back to the video."

A mime comes to the center with an official's uniform, forming the shape of a whistle, and blows it loud. The sound can be audibly heard. He gestures his hands pushing the Gooney Clowns back "fifteen-yard penalty" he signs to them.

The clown in the interview room pauses the video. "Who does that? Who throws a flag in a dance battle?" The clowns, for one reason or another, go back fifteen yards. The battle continues on video with further comical antics.

The White-Out Squad and Shifty Eyes are running to the scene. By the time they arrive, the only thing they witness are piles of salt on the floor. Some piles are straight black while the others are glowing fluorescent green. With the witness around before he gets there, he again tries to cover the scene.

"This is a social experiment of your brain on drugs. Don't do drugs, and stay in school, kids," as they return the scene back to what it once was. Vacuuming up the salt on the floor, covering up any paint leftover, the White-Out Squad leaves no trace.

The leader of the clown tells the interviewer, "Did you see what happened?"

"What do you mean?" says the reporter.

"Never mind…" utters the clown with apparent frustration across his face.

"It's just everyone loves the mimes. Everybody hates clowns. Why they hate us? I don't know but they do."

"Well, there is coulrophobia, which can include mimes."

"Look at the band Kiss, they look like mimes. Everybody loves mimes. Even kids hate us." He gets evidently emotional with tears coming to his eyes. "We just want to spread joy to the world," he continues.

"Wow, you're taking this personally. You know, we interviewed the Mime Gang Crew as well," says the reporter.

"Oh, you did, huh. And what did they say?"

"They said they see you like family."

"Well, they don't treat us like family," ending the interview broadcast there.

Back at the station, Shifty Eyes and his team seem to be losing quite a bit of morale. A member of the White-Out Squad throws the paint rod on the floor.

"I quit! Fuck this shit." Shifty Eyes steps up to him promptly, getting close to his face.

"Remember your contract. The knowledge you have puts you in more danger for quitting rather than staying. If you snitch, you know what happens."

"You know what I think about your contract?" the man says, flashing the middle finger at him as he walks away.

*****

Added trouble for Zvmcx awaits as federal agents now head their way to his apartment.

"How does a guy disappear for over five years?" says one agent to another.

"It does say here he was homeless, so perhaps just unregistered whereabouts?"

"Maybe he was just living with the rats." He laughed to his companion. But little did he know he may have been closer to the truth than he may have realized. They go up the door and begin to knock, but they are interrupted by none other than Shifty Eyes.

"Hello, hi, we are taking over the case here."

Zvmcx peers from his window seeing the three outside. He quickly dashes out the back window upon hearing the first knock. Running through the alleyway up the fire escape onto a rooftop, two people, awfully similar in appearance to Zvmcx, Zavior and Vicky, begin pleading with him as he walks to the edge looking at a building across a gap.

"You can do it, just go!" they tell Zvmcx. He runs and jumps, crashing through the window of an apartment belonging to a Latina woman. She swiftly hits him over the head with a broomstick, chasing him out of the property. With sirens not far from him, a memory pops into his head. *The mole people*, he thinks of himself, now knowing where he can turn.

You see, Zvmcx has been there before and built quite a relationship with these "mole people"—a society of "homeless" men and women who've built almost a civilization within the subway tunnels underneath, only to be accessed by the homeless who have been given the key. Five jars of peanut butter is that key. Persuading the rats that guard it to step aside, allowing passage. The leader of the moles told Zvmcx himself, "You're always welcome here."

The mimes watching Zvmcx carefully through the exposed graffiti see him entering the subway and feel it is safe to follow, so they do so. They greet Zvmcx as they step through the rats. The mimes don't seem to bother them at all.

One mime mimes to Zvmcx. "This would be perfect for your hidden lair."

"Mole people are highly sophisticated homeless people. They choose to live in their own society," says Zvmcx before running in the leader of the moles once more.

"Hello, Zvmcx!" a boisterous yet warm greeting is heard, that of an old friend. After a brief embrace, he continues, "Oh, I know why you're here," as the mimes sit there in confusion.

"Remember, the rats are all over the city, and I never forgot one of my own. Now here, if you'll follow me, I have something for you." He brings him over to a box. Inside the box is a black gimp-like spandex suit and gas mask. The gas mask, however, is no normal gas mask. Its design is very cartoony, looking very much like a winking face.

"What is this?" says Zvmcx.

"Every superhero has a costume."

"I'm not a superhero though."

The mimes are now chiming in mime. "You can become more than what you are."

On the other side of things, a not-so-warm welcome greets Shifty Eyes. The CEO of NXC is really hammering him, physically beating him with his fist.

"I've paid you so much money to get rid of this problem." Bruised by the beating, Shifty Eyes puts his hands up very submissively, backing up. He stutters each word as he begins to speak. "Wai…wai…wait…wait…I-I…I know someone who can fix it," he says.

"Get them. You can leave now," says the CEO to Shifty Eyes.

CHAPTER 5

Ayoung man is getting beaten up in the middle of the night. Harsh slurs fly at him regarding his sexual orientation—"fag," "twink"—and anything of that sort hurls in the air as four men continue to attack the one. But even in the dark, there's always a superhero at bay. Zvmcx approaches from behind the corner of the building. He looks and studies the situation, breaking down how to fight the group in front of him.

"This is gang combat fighting. You can't fight like normal hand-to-hand. You have to immobilize, improvise, then show off," he says, reminding himself what he's learned. He runs into the altercation narrating as he does each move, pinning one man to the floor, *immobilizing,* as he breaks the arm of one. Another one pulls a gun, pointing it at Zvmcx.

Surprising him, "Improvise," he says as he grabs the gun hand flipping the man over his shoulder.

"Show off," he says. After disarming the man, he performs a backflip off the wall, kicking another man in the head. Looking around, he sees a woman recording in the background.

"Cuer-all. Do you suffer from unexplainable hallucinations? Try Cuer-all. Without Cuer-all, I was unable to think. My thoughts were all over the place."

A TV commercial plays; a clown in the lead excitedly stands as the narration describes the drug.

"I knew I was gonna be famous. Look at me, in a commercial," he says. Employees outside of the frame hand him a bucket.

"What's this for?" he asks.

"Cuer-all may cause depression, tearing of the eyes, fatigue." The clown quickly becomes depressed, begins crying, and gets tired.

"Wait, what's happening?" he asks.

"Weakness, constipation, diarrhea, increase appetite, decrease appetite." Unable to hold the bucket and dropping it, he sits on it, dropping his pants because he has to use the restroom. He attempts to poop, to no avail. Suddenly, too much avail with immense diarrhea. His stomach shrinks as it feels empty and hunger takes, then promptly becomes full and bloated as he's no longer hungry. "Dehydration, weight loss, spontaneous combustion. If you experience any of these, please call. Sideforia, which may cause exploding eardrums…" They continue down the list of side effects as he experiences them all. Good thing they hired a clown for this commercial certainly.

An interviewer is interviewing a former employee from the NXC.

"I used to hear things," he says.

"Like what, exactly?" the interviewer asks.

"They seem to be going after someone named Zvmcx. They were obsessed with this guy and his buddy, 'unforgettable Dr. Z.' In all missions, I've never seen him," he explains. The reporter is asking further about his opinion of Shifty Eyes as well as he seems to be a foreperson in public relations for the NXC. The employee describes him as "PBA," which he later defined as "professional bullshit artist," causing the reporter to chuckle a little bit.

"Do you have any regrets?"

"No, I actually think I left just in time. There was this really creepy dude. I get goose bumps talking about him. He literally looks like a TV set for eyes projecting the past and future at the same time. They called him 'Timeless Man.'" The employee asks the reporter a final question before leaving.

"About that witness protection you promised me?" The live interview cuts off.

The greatest time machine ever invented was the mind. "Able to remember the past, capable to manipulate the present, and strong enough to foresee the future," a phrase once said by some seemingly unimportant crazy guy, but wise words nonetheless.

Shifty Eyes is discussing with Timeless Man. "You owe me," says Shifty Eyes.

"I don't owe anybody. You forgot your place, let me remind you" Timeless Man says in retaliation, staring directly into Shifty Eyes's...well, eyes. He projects an image going all the way back into his childhood.

* * * * *

A young Shifty Eyes plays inside his house. Other kids come to his window making fun of him from outside.

"Hey, crazy eyes, what's the matter? Your mother won't let you out to play? Ha ha." He closes the blinds, running to his mother, tears filling his eyes.

"Those kids keep making fun of me," he says to his mother. His mother bends down on to her knees, looking at him face to face.

"They just don't know how special you are," she says.

"I don't want to be special." He runs away to his room slamming his door. While on his floor, he grabs a laser by his bed. It seems as though he's looking to control the sporadicity of his eyes, pointing the laser, focusing in on it.

Timeless Man now shifts his view to six months later. The kids are still screaming into his window.

"Crazy eyes, crazy eyes, crazy eyes" as Shifty Eyes still tends to his laser, able to see it move even as he flicks his wrist, the laser gliding across the wall, almost appearing to be in slow motion. Some more time passes, and a young Shifty Eyes walks outside with his baseball equipment. A bat and some gloves sit in his bags.

As he meets the kids outside, "Oh, finally allowed outside, huh? Which way you lookin' at? Can't tell," a boy says to Shifty Eyes.

"Let's play," Shifty Eyes says.

"Whatever, crazy eyes," the boy says. He pitches the ball to Shifty Eyes, and the next thing he notices is waking up with a baseball next to him with massive swelling on his forehead.

With Shifty Eyes standing over the boy, grabbing him by the hair, he says, "It's Shifty Eyes, not crazy eyes." Shifty Eyes comes out of the trance from the Timeless Man with tears welled up in his eyes.

"I never break a promise," says Timeless Man as he walks through the door.

*****

Zvmcx is heading back to his hiding space as he sees people running from rooftop to rooftop. Walking by on a rainy night, everything around him appears motionless for a few seconds. Paying no mind to it, at this point, he reaches his hideout. Turning on the TV, alive broadcast explains the newly found alien species that has landed on earth. The Cinaji is described as a bio-celestial being genetically modified for greatness.

A person on the investigation team grabs the microphone and looks very evidently brainwashed but speaks, "We come in peace, don't shoot. Peace out, deuces!" dropping the mic and walking off camera. The news anchor, stunned and confused, goes on to the next story.

"Just in, a new gay superhero named Zvmcx stops hate crime in the act. A live video is coming right now, viewer discretion is advised." Zvmcx stands up as he sees himself on TV. The footage looks blurry. Flattered, he stands.

"To the woman who sent the video, do you have anything you'd like to say?"

"I don't care if he's gay or not. I'll turn him straight."

"Cuer-all, have you been experiencing…" The message is cut in half by the interrupting clown.

"I'm suing all you mutha fuckers for making me do that dumbass commercial. Get this shit off." He reaches for the camera.

"Cuer-all, proudly funded by the NXC."

CHAPTER 6

APPROACHING STARS

Two older men are fishing on a boat. One of the men is reading a book and utters a question that's hard for him to understand.

"If men are from Mars and women are from Venus…where do gay people come from?" a joke that either emphasizes the age or the lack of life experience these two men have outside their fishing boat.

*****

Far above the clouds where the gods play dice and far past even the rings of Saturn, what may be seen as a shooting star to some may be more than what's bargained for. Deep beyond the cosmos, what appears to be a star was actually a spaceship. Darwin has spoken about animals and creatures in evolution using this to survive but never to this extent—adaptation. The ship seems to be morphing and adapting as they travel through, not knowing their intention is surely frightening, to say the least.

A scientist being interviewed for the NXC program has seen enough, it seems.

As the broadcast starts, he utters, "Can I go back to work now? There's an alien race coming that I have to prepare for." He steals a bowl of plantains on the interviewer's desk and walks away.

Zvmcx, sitting upon a rooftop looking over the city, sees young people jumping from building to building in a display of beautiful acrobatics. In awe of this, being something he's never seen before, Zvmcx stops one, yelling "Yo!"

A familiar man in a lab coat. That's right. The man who stopped the purse thief, Dr. Z.

"Yo, you're that gay superhero everyone keeps talking about, right?" Dr. Z says.

"I'm not…I'm no…"

"Look, bro, I don't want no problem. I'm just saying that shit was dope. What did you stop me for?" Zvmcx is blushing through his mask.

"What was that thing you were doing? Can you teach me?"

"What, parkour? Free running? Sure," assuring Zvmcx that he will teach him this new skill that will undoubtedly be useful in chasing bad guys and doing superhero duties.

* * * * *

A few young people are on a basketball court dancing. We know what this does at this point. Not too far, a mural of an angel on a building becomes the opening point for mimes to enter. A young boy tying his shoes by the mural bears witness to the group as they come out. Staring in awe, confusion and fear become stuck in his mind.

A person from the court, somehow unfamiliar with the mimes, presses them from the court.

"Yo, you in the wrong area!" A female mime from the group claps her hands. The clapping continues in the background. She pops and locks to the opposing woman, in sync with each clap. The pace of the background clapping switches along with the dancing style. The mimes all slide toward the court as if they are being pushed on ice. Some mimes run to the left and right gathering people to witness, others are dancing around the lead women, while a few are *playing* the music. The music scratches to halt while the majority of the mimes freeze. Except for one. The one mobile mime picks up something and does a few practice swings as if he is a professional baseball player. He walks behind a mime and swings his hands with incredible force. The mime in front of him shatters, turning into the black salt below.

"Yo, they gotta be fucking freaks!" says the woman on the court in the opposing crew. The leader of the Mime Gang Crew dribbles an invisible basketball with immense skill, throwing his hands up like a free throw with nothing on his hand. Though nothing comes out of his hands, the net still swishes as if a ball passed through. The newly formed crowd runs to the mimes in excitement and attempts to embrace. As the group collides into the mimes, they vanish to the black salt on the floor again.

Promptly after the spectacle, a news reporter runs quickly to an onlooker. Someone must've tipped them off to the event that transpired.

"Tell me, sir, what just happened here?" says the reporter to a viewer.

"I'll tell you what just happened. I just saw the illest dance crew ever in NYC. That's all I gotta say," the man says excitedly as he looks at the camera.

The White-Out Squad van pulls up to the scene closing off the area, and Shifty Eyes steps out. Looking to cover the scene again, he walks up to the cameraman and reporter preparing to lie through his teeth.

"We have reason to believe that an airborne disease has made it to the US. This area has to be quarantined. We have free Cuer-all to those who might be experiencing any hallucinations. Please take one as you leave." The squad hands out pills to those lining up to leave the zone. Once the last person leaves, the White-Out Squad cleans the area in its entirety, vacuuming the salt left over and sweeping out any debris.

"What have we here?" On a milk carton being swept by White-Out Squad lies a picture of their old comrade. "Missing" is the only thing written on the carton.

"I haven't seen that method of search for years."

Zvmcx is in the midst of a lesson with Dr. Z now. As he jumps from one building to another, making their way through the city,

Zvmcx feels a presence behind him—Timeless Man. Timeless Man touches the top of Zvmcx's head. He begins convulsing and falls to his back until he sees it. With more untouched graffiti on the roof, he crawls toward it slowly yet as quickly as he can. Timeless Man seems to indulge in the glee of his prey seemingly defeated. As Zvmcx gets closer a hand reaches from the graffiti, Zvmcx reaches back to the hand until the two hands meet quickly, grasping each other. As the hand of the mimes pull him into the graffiti, the unlikely safe haven, Timeless Man reaches to the graffiti, to no avail, touching the solid wall behind it.

"I know you, who finally presents itself. A creature born of chaos."

The two fishermen back on the boat see the "shooting star" plummeting toward the earth. The impact of the water capsizes the boat, flipping them over. They breach the surface holding on to the overturned boat as a floatation device.

"So that's where starfish come from, huh?" he jokingly says to the other fisherman.

"You're an idiot," he says in response while laughing.

CHAPTER 7

WHO OR WHAT ARE THEY?

Shifty Eyes and Timeless Man are having an *interaction* with a homeless man. The two begin beating the man badly in an attempt to obtain information. Timeless Man pulls out the tool of his trade. A ball, similar to a psychic's future seeing ball, is used by Timeless Man to force another worldly experience to others. Holding the ball up to the man's face, as what can only be described as a near death experience, he overtakes the man.

The immense fear shown on his face brings a smile to Timeless Man as finally he speaks, "Okay, okay, okay, I heard a rumor…just a rumor of an underground society." The two smile as a lead on their target has now been found.

"We are about to initiate first contact with the alien ship about to enter our atmosphere," a reporter says as they broadcast NXC news. Two opposing crowds find themselves gathering behind the reporter. One side chanting "What about God!" and "The end is near!" The other crowd yelling "Peace and love! We accept you," speaking to the aliens directly before they're even sighted. The reporter stands in front of the camera visibly frightened but attempts to maintain her composure.

"Okay, they're about to enter the atmosphere." The ship, breaching the atmosphere, crashes into the water. Everybody stands and watches the ship eject itself out of the water and brings itself closer to land. It approaches the land with great speed and kicks up dirt as it lands.

The ship, in closer detail, reveals more of its design. Scales layer the outside of the ship, changing size and color, matching its surroundings before their very eyes.

"Do you come in peace?" the onlookers wait patiently after military personnel ask that question. The ship changes yet again before their eyes, forming a sort of platform it seems, a stage if you will. People lie there confused as what looks like droplets of light begin to fall from the sky. To their disbelief, what comes out of the ship is remarkably human in appearance.

Stepping on to the stage, they respond, "We do come in peace," but not in any single solid voice. It sounds like an amalgamation of radio broadcasts. From songs to host, they combine the voices to form the sentence needed. This must be how they speak.

The crowd, exuberant with the news of peaceful oncoming, yells in shock, "Yooo, they come in peace," says one man.

"This is crazy!" says another excitedly. A man in a lab coat, presumably a scientist, cuts through the crowd and stands in front of the newly placed boundary tape set by government officials.

"What is your purpose here?" the scientist asks.

A creature responds, "To show you the path of greatness," in the same robotic combination used before.

A civilian quickly butts in, "What about God!"

The alien responds back, "We actually drove past him on the way here. He asked if we would show you the path of greatness. He's a good guy." The aliens begin to speak to each other. The crowd can't understand what's being said but "these people are crazy, maybe we should go back" is what one alien told another. The aliens begin playing music. The music is very earthlike, as if made by earthlings themselves. The group introduce themselves. Cinaji is what they call themselves. The music imbues calmness into the listeners directly, almost against their will.

"We would like to see your spaceship," the lead scientist asks the Cinaji. The Cinaji warmly welcome them into the ship. The scientist takes his team and leads them into the ship observing the fascinating technologies it has to offer.

"You can come whenever you like," the Cinaji say as they play music in the background. The team who was once walking cautiously through the unfamiliar space have a sudden wave of calm as the music puts them almost in a hypnotic state.

The White-Out Squad, using the information gathered before going searching, enter a tunnel their lead may have clued to. Timeless Man and Shifty Eyes watch from a distance watching the infiltration. After the crew enters the tunnel, they are promptly chased out by rats. What they don't see is one of the men fall and the rats attack relentlessly like piranha, eating the man.

"What are you doing? Get back there," Shifty Eyes tells a squad member.

"You go down there. They got these man-eating rats."

"There's no man-eating rats," Shifty Eyes says as he grabs a flashlight and heads into the tunnel himself promptly to be chased by the rats with one stuck on his ear as he runs out frantically, giving some of his men and Timeless Man quite a laugh.

Shifty Eyes, now in front of the CEO, fills him in on the situation they had experienced previously.

"It's virtually impossible to get into the mole society," Shifty Eyes says.

"Well, you two better figure it out. I pay you both way too much to have nothing," the CEO says in response.

"This has nothing to do with me. You guys called *me* to help," Timeless Man argued. They're kicked out of the room.

Shifty Eyes looks down at the floor pondering what to do next. Stress riddles his face, revealing the emotion he feels inside, until he remembers something. In the past, he recalls a receipt that was by the tunnel of the society during his interrogation. The receipt has one item on it—peanut butter. Shortly after the discovery, the NXC flex their authority prohibiting any purchase of peanut butter in any quantity.

CHAPTER 8

NEW TOOLS OF THE TRADE

Members of the Mime Gang Crew stand atop of a roof. With telescoping monocular in hand scanning the buildings, surprised by what he sees, he looks back into the window.

"Give me sight beyond sight," the mimes see this person's mouth out loud. Then with a snap of his jaw, the person in the building quickly turns, focusing in on the mimes.

"Is that Liono?"

Liono, inside the building, grabs the sword. A member of the White-Out Squad shouts out.

"Liono."

"Hey, gimme that," he says.

Shifty Eyes and the White-Out Squad officer approach Liono. He throws the sword to his right. A woman busts out the door with almost supernatural speeds, catching the sword and running past some of the White-Out Squad and around to the door. Quickly realizing the door is locked, she turns again bolting through to the back window. With eyes set on the fire escape, as she heads past Shifty Eyes. He's able to read the movement, sticking his foot out and tripping her.

"Ah, so you thought you were that fast, huh?" He picked up the sword from her hand. The Mime Gang Crew, still witnessing from the rooftop, mimes.

"They got our kind in there."

Zvmcx is walking through a field. In his head, however, he keeps hearing a message.

"Come on, follow the voice. You're headed in the right direction," the voice says repeatedly, leading Zvmcx straight to the Cinaji. Upon his arrival, he is shocked to find someone there with him—Dr. Z.

"What are you doing?" Zvmcx asks.

"I was just following a voice."

"So was I. But why?"

The Cinaji speak up, "You have a higher calling. Keep following. You must follow to fulfill your destiny." The two get into the Cinaji's spaceship. Inside, they see a strange creature. Tiny bull-bodied but frog-faced animals. Horns protrude from the top of their head. It seems as though the horn is used to ram things that angered them. Two of these frogs attempt to ram each other but miss. The poor, silly creatures, as they miss and continue, one rams into Cinaji while he is attempting to shake the hands of the two. The Cinaji kicks the creature onto its back in frustration. Slowly but surely, it flips back over. Zvmcx and Dr. Z are visibly confused as the Cinaji cordially invites them inside.

The Cinaji seat them inside, feeding them a strange meal. The meal itself seems to give Zvmcx strength as his muscles are slightly larger. They also bring to the table two more gifts, handing Zvmcx a staff that is extremely heavy, but with his newfound strength, he's able to carry it. Dr. Z gets a pair of futuristic goggles VR headsets that allow him to see the short-term future.

"You two carry the fate of how this world ends," the Cinaji warns them.

* * * * *

In front of the NXC, a large crowd is formed. The CEO stands by the window overlooking the crowd. With anger in his face, he questions himself. "How can I spend all this money, and it has not been dealt with already?" But out loud to Shifty Eyes in the room, he says, "Why are all these people here?"

Shifty Eyes responds with the same level of disappointment. "I'll take care of it." Stepping outside the building, he sees the Cinaji performing a song.

Shifty Eyes directs his words toward the crowd. "Why are you guys even here? Half of you don't even work here." Seeing signs from "I love you" to "Bring back Free Taco Night," he stands there in confusion, addressing the crowd section by section.

* * * * *

A Gooney Clown member hitches a ride from Jersey to New York, a sandwich in his seat for lunch. While finally in New York, he decides it's time to enjoy his lunch, a PB and J. As he walks by a police officer, the police officer stops.

Sniffing the air as he stands behind our friend, Mr. Clown, the officer walks up to the clown.

"What I do now?" he says to the officer.

"What do you have here?" he says, grabbing the sandwich. "You know this is illegal in the state of New York, right?"

"Uh-oh" is the clown's only response.

Sitting inside a courtroom now, with a tiny umbrella to block the bright lights, "How do you plead?" the judge asks.

"Not guilty" is the response given. The judge stands up in frustration.

"You know, I deal with punks like you all day. The evidence is right here." He is pointing to a picture. The first picture shows the truck that he got out of. A second picture shows that when he uncovered the bed of the truck, it revealed tons of peanut butter.

"Well, I didn't know he had the truck full—" the clown says. The judge continues to describe the disrespect he feels from the way the clown is dressed to the fact that he has an umbrella. Dropping the gavel, sentencing the clown to jail. Where the answer to the question "what are you in for" in his case is simply "peanut butter."

CHAPTER 9

THE NXC EXPOSES THEMSELVES

The NXC is having a large crowd formed in front of the building. It's time for them to explain to the people who they are and what they do. Shifty Eyes steps in front of the crowds and invites them in, giving them a tour of the building, showing the group and the cameras that come with it around.

"These servers control 85 percent of the Internet to protect society from threats. They are protected by an asymmetrical algorithm. We have the best of the best hackers try to crack through our firewall daily. If you believe you can, please feel free to try. No, seriously, we haven't been able to get into the system for fifteen years," Shifty Eyes says, boasting continuously about the security. After the statement is broadcasted, the server goes live. The screens in the building now are displaying something different. *Signal transfer from an outside source. The mothership is obtaining control,* is displayed as the mothership of the Cinaji is gaining control of all the computers in the world.

Dr. Z is unknowingly in trouble. Lurking behind the interconnected spectrum in the absence of time and following his every move, Timeless Man is planning his attack. You see, he knew Dr. Z's every movement down to a science. He knew he worked for FedEx part-time, practiced parkour, and went to the gym Tuesdays and Thursdays in the afternoon. So the only free time he actually has is

7:45–9:00 p.m., and that's when it happens. Timeless Man traps Dr. Z in a parallel space continuum bubble.

"Where is Zvmcx?" a creepy voice asks Dr. Z. Zvmcx appears right on cue with his new staff hitting Timeless Man, which in turn collapses the bubble. They begin to fight, but as the moves are thrown at Timeless Man, he somehow projects moves into the past, dodging them. Yet again, the Cinaji's gifts come to use. Dr. Z's goggles predict how he plans to move about one to three seconds before the move is initiated. Armed with his slingshot, Dr. Z shoots where his head is. Zvmcx reacts to the slingshot ammo, and with his staff that alters its own time, he is able to hit Timeless Man one more time before sending him running.

"It's not over. It's only just begun," Timeless Man says before he vanishes through a door.

The White-Out Squad continues to complain about working conditions. They couldn't stand the amount of labor the union dues just won't cover.

"We demand changes," an employee says.

Shifty Eyes responds, "What's with all the hostility?"

"Trying to take down Zvmcx cost Antonio's life. He got eaten by rats. I think that's enough. We're not equipped to handle these situations," the employee says. This statement struck Shifty Eyes. It appears he does care for the employees. With a sigh, he gets up, walks over to a filing cabinet, and pulls out a large stack of paper, handing one to each of the employees in the room. It's the contracts they've signed.

"Turn to page 467," Shifty Eyes says. "See here, never mind the fact that it's in my handwriting. If you quit, you'll be locked up for the rest of your life. No one will know you existed," he tells them. So much for care. The employees go back to work.

The NXC aren't the only ones investigating Zvmcx. The FBI agents who were investigating before haven't given up the case as easily as assumed. Inside their headquarters, you see a collection of pictures laid out on the table. From the homeless man playing the drums in the beginning, the Mime Gang Crew and Gooney Clowns, the Cinaji, NXC, White-Out Squad, Zvmcx, and Dr. Z all laid out across the table.

"All these people are connected to one man," their boss repeats what they say, sarcastic in tone.

"So are you gonna give us the go ahead to take down both crews?"

The boss waves his hand at them. "Sure, sure, sure. Go ahead," he says, waving them away from his work station.

CHAPTER 10

With ever growing fame and popularity of the Cinaji, they find themselves on a talk show.

"You guys survived on earth for three days and have close to half a billion followers on social media. If there's anyone that knows anything about showbiz, it's you. It's actually amazing. We have a couple of fans that have a few questions," the host tells the Cinaji before bringing the fans on. Compliments flood the lines one after another.

"I'm your biggest fan" by some. "I think you're hot, let's start a new species" is said by others. The recent uproar being directed toward the Cinaji with the most "feminine figure," within three days of arrival, the following they've gathered is unmatched. After the fans' questions/comments, they sing a one-to-one cover of a popular song and sign off the show.

Zvmcx and Dr. Z both sit in hiding, looking at each other.

"You ready?" Zvmcx asks Dr. Z. Dr. Z nods in response, and they begin. Leaving their hiding spot, they run across the rooftop jumping from one to another, leaving behind a tail of FBI agents chasing them. Zvmcx and Dr. Z reach their headquarters and meet an array of new characters. Misio, a baby-like fellow, throws a Pamper on the floor; Cap, a sad-looking man who wields a sledge-hammer;

and Xjr, the most intelligent looking one—turtleneck, glasses, etc.—is the only one to ask when they walk in.

"Who are you guys?"

In a separate location, the Mime Gang Crew runs steadily, also being chased by law enforcement. The mimes jump down the building and all pile into this mimed out car. As they're speeding off down the block and on to another, a parade of sorts is on the road.

"Oh my god, it's the Mime Gang Crew," onlookers say as they are not very inconspicuous, driving an invisible car and such. The crowd opens up, letting the crew pass, seeing the commotion behind.

The crew, finally able to abandon the "car," run into an abandoned building.

"We have you surrounded," blares loudly outside from the megaphones. The White-Out Squad arrives on the scene in an attempt to disrupt the police force at hand.

"You have no jurisdiction here," he says.

The FBI responds promptly, "Fuck off, this is our case now."

"I don't care," Shift Eyes pleads with them. "You're not fully equipped to handle this." They push Shifty Eyes to the side, signaling the law enforcement to rush the building, killing the lights of the building, walking in equipped with lights and thermal scopes. Through the scopes, the officers see the Mime Gang Crew. A cackling laugh in the dark stops the officers. The Gooney Clowns glowing fluorescently in the building rush the officers, beating them up with ease, apprehending them, and seizing the weapons.

"So what? Are you like family now?" asks an agent who lays there tied up.

"We've been family," says the clown, turning some of the lights back on.

"You guys have had beef since day one?"

"Families fight sometimes. Eventually, you get over it," mimed the leader of the Mime Gang Crew. As the laughter continues between the two groups becoming one in solidarity, it seems to be abruptly short-lived. On the clown's head, a laser is seen for only moments. A white paintball shoots him. As he drops, the lights surrounding them drop as well, seemingly shut off yet again by the White-Out Squad now. The Gooney Clowns being the only group to express glowing in the dark capability is no longer the case. As the room becomes encased in darkness, it is revealed that the mimes glow also. More police officers storm the building.

"Get him!" they say, referring to the leader. The leader who visibly stands there upset, counters the charge, beating every officer as they enter. He picks up the body camera and looks into it, wearing the emotion of sadness ever so evidently on his face.

ABOUT THE AUTHOR

Under the pen name Dr. Z this story is written as the interpretation of real world events. Written and co-written by brothers through phone calls over the course of many years. This is part 1 of the dramatic story of Zvmcx. The amalgamation of several characters to be introduced which represent a small part of the author's personality, as you go through this journey more of the truth will be unveiled as to who Zvmcx is, the role that society had in creating this, and whether or not he becomes the hero he wants to be, or the monster that society tells him he is.